Liu and the Bird

A Journey in Chinese Calligraphy

Written and illustrated by
Catherine Louis

Calligraphy by **Feng Xiao Min**

Translated by Sibylle Kazeroid

North-South Books

New York / London

night

moon

That **night**, the **moon** came in through the window.
I was dreaming of Grandfather.
He was talking to me—his lips were forming my name,
Liu—but I didn't hear what he said.

It wasn't yet daylight when I got up. I had decided to go see Grandfather, on the other side of the mountains. I tied my things in a bundle and set off on my way. A **star** guided me.

star

child

After walking for a few hours, I came across a **child** on the bank of a **river**. He was drawing on the rocks with the burnt end of a stick.

river

stick

I asked him which way to go. He told me to follow the river.
And he gave me his **stick**.

The river led me to a **forest**. I walked through it
in the shade of the tall **trees**. The **treetops**
swayed gently, murmuring my name: Li-u, Li-u, Li-u.

tree

forest

treetop

When I left the forest, I came to a **crossroads**. Should I go straight? Turn right? Left? I threw the stick that the child had given me into the air, and when it fell, the point showed me which way to take.

crossroads

field

woman

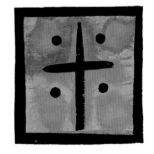

rice

The path took me through **fields**.
By noontime, I was very hungry.
I passed a **woman** who had just gathered
her **rice**.
She shared her meal with me and gave me
a sheaf of rice.

I set off again on my way.

I saw a **man** at **rest** under a tree. He showed me a bird that was flying above the mountains and said I should **follow** it.

man

rest

follow

mountains

The **mountains** were so high! And the snow on them glittered like the sun!

When I reached the top of the mountain, the bird had disappeared, but it had left tracks in the **snow**, and a **feather** to show me the way.

My **feet** were frozen, but I kept walking.

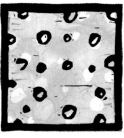

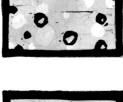

snow

feather

foot

On the other side of the mountain, the **sun** was **shining**. Near a thicket of **bamboo**, an old man was making himself a parasol.

"I recognize you," he said. "You're Liu. You are going to see your grandfather, aren't you?"

And he showed me a shortcut through the fields.

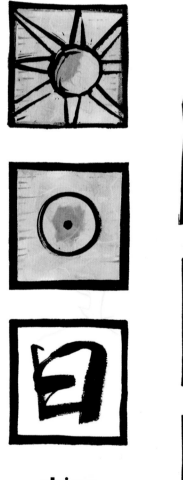

sun

shine

bamboo

draw

see

Finally I could **see** Grandfather's house.
He was sitting at his worktable, **drawing**.

He was not surprised to see me.
"I was waiting for you," he told me. "I knew you would hear my call. Because the voice of **love** can be heard from far away."

love

Grandfather gave me a paintbrush and asked me to tell him about my journey. Not with words, but with pictures. Not with my **mouth**, but with my **hands**.

mouth

hand

I drew the child, the woman, the man under his tree, the old man in the bamboo thicket.

countryside

I drew the bird, too.
And suddenly, it flew off the page
and disappeared into the **countryside**.

Since that day, I continue to fill the garden of my dreams with **birds**.

bird

Activity Ideas

Pictures are at the root of all writing, no matter what culture the writing comes from. This book opens a window onto the world of pictographs, symbols, and letters. Using the evolution of Chinese script, children can trace the origins of words, from pictures to abstract printed characters to the letters of today's alphabets. Starting with simple sketches that depict the sun, the moon, and humans, children learn how signs are combined to make more complex concepts, such as the way sun and moon together can symbolize the word for day.

The following activities invite children to participate in the art of writing and painting. They can be shared by children and adults, and can be done at home or in school.

Illustrated Writing

Materials: index cards, colored pencils, markers, crayons, or paints and brushes

Tell stories and everyday experiences with your own drawings, inspired by the Chinese characters in this book. Use the index cards to make a picture gallery. Draw or paint a picture on each card to represent words, expressions, or people. Cards can then be grouped by themes like family, your room, homes, your city, a vacation, a school trip, a visit to the zoo, a train ride, etc.

Variation: Make your own alphabet. Make a drawing for each letter with a word that starts with that letter. For example, draw an ant for A, a bear for B, etc. Write the complete word for each letter on the back of the card. Then make up stories, and use the cards to tell them.

Bilingual Picture Alphabet Memory Game

Materials: index cards, colored pencils, markers, crayons, or paints and brushes

Draw or paint a picture on one side of the card and write the corresponding word in English and in another language on the back of the card. For example: feather, love, moon, night, star. Then play a game with the cards by laying them picture side up and taking turns trying to remember the name in both languages.

Make Up Your Own Symbols

Materials: paper, pencils, crayons, markers, or paints

Start with your own name. Turn the letters into figures. If your name has meaning on its own, it can easily be made into an image. For example, the last name "Fisher" could be drawn as a fish, or fisherman. You could also make the letters by drawing things you like, such as hobbies, games, or your favorite food or snack. The number 7 could be symbolized by seven dots in the shape of a seven. Initials could be outlined and decorated.

Flashlight Picture Magic

Materials: flashlight, paper, pens, scissors, clear tape

Hold a flashlight so the head (or light end) is facedown on a piece of paper. Now trace around the head of the flashlight with a pencil. Carefully cut it out, cutting just inside of the line so that the paper will fit flat on the glass when you are finished. Now draw or trace a picture, letter, or shape onto the paper and carefully cut it out. Tape your cutout onto the head of the flashlight. Darken the room, turn on the flashlight, and get ready to be amazed.

Variation: Group activity

Give each child a flashlight and have each create his or her own paper shape. After taping the shapes onto their flashlights, darken the room and use all the lighted shapes, either one at a time, or all together, to tell a story, flashing the shapes on the wall as you go along.

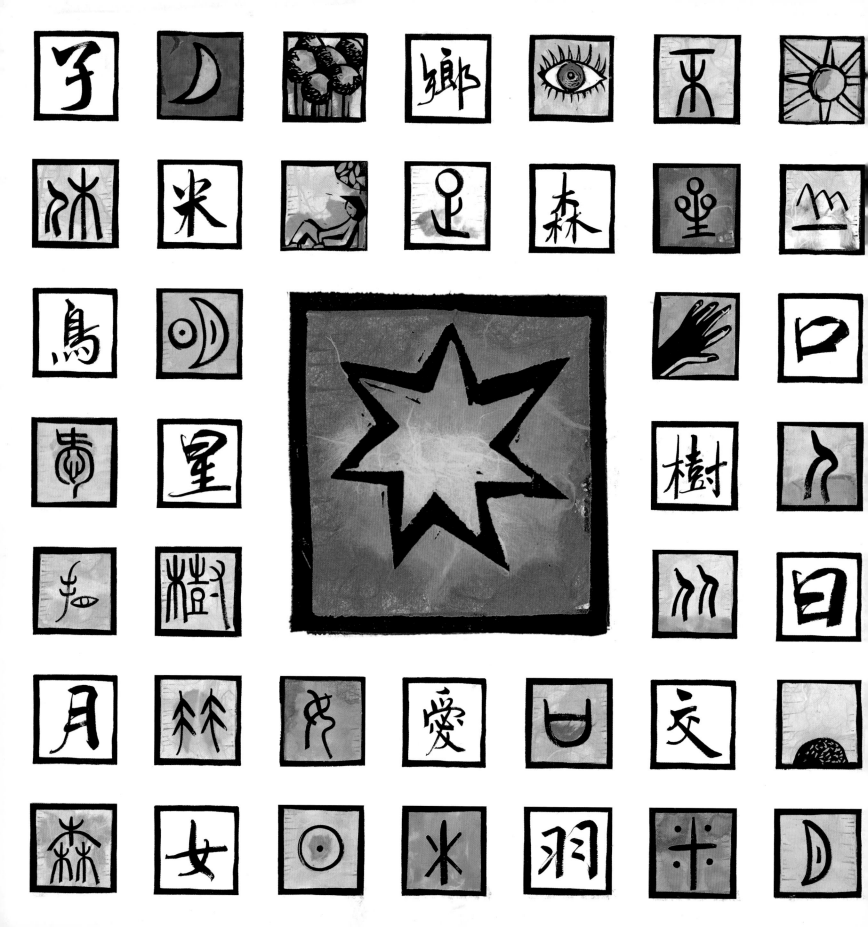